Mogie
The Heart of the House

This book is dedicated to all the children and
families of the world who understand
the love of a special furry friend.

atheneum

ATHENEUM BOOKS FOR YOUNG READERS
An imprint of Simon & Schuster Children's Publishing Division
1230 Avenue of the Americas, New York, New York 10020
For information about special discounts for bulk purchases, please contact
Simon & Schuster Special Sales at 1-866-506-1949 or business@simonandschuster.com.
The Simon & Schuster Speakers Bureau can bring authors to your live event.
For more information or to book an event,
contact the Simon & Schuster Speakers Bureau at 1-866-248-3049
or visit our website at www.simonspeakers.com.
Book design by Sonia Chaghatzbanian
The text for this book is set in Abadi.
The illustrations for this book are rendered in pencil and charcoal, and digitally.
Manufactured in China
0314 SCP
First Edition
2 4 6 8 10 9 7 5 3 1
Library of Congress Cataloging-in-Publication Data
Appelt, Kathi, 1954-
Mogie : the heart of the house / Kathi Appelt ; illustrated by Marc Rosenthal. — First edition.
p. cm
Summary: A rambunctious puppy finds a home at the Ronald McDonald House, a place that houses sick
children and their families while they undergo treatment.
ISBN 978-1-4424-8054-4 (hardcover) — ISBN 978-1-4424-8055-1 (ebook) [1. Dogs—Fiction. 2.
Animals—Infancy—Fiction. 3. Sick—Fiction. 4. Ronald McDonald House Charities—Fiction.] I. Rosenthal,
Marc, 1949- illustrator. II. Title.
PZ7.A6455Mo 2014
[E]—dc23
2013018100

Mogie
The Heart of
the House

by Kathi Appelt   *illustrated by* Marc Rosenthal

Atheneum Books for Young Readers
New York London Toronto Sydney New Delhi

Right smack in the heart of the Big City is a very special house.

It has high-to-the-sky ceilings
and large, cushy sofas. It has a
well-stocked library and a big,
big kitchen.

It has an indoor
tree house and an
enormous fireplace.

NAOMI'S TREE HOUSE

The families who stay at the special house
come from all over the world. They bring
their children with them.

Including . . . Gage.
Gage was once a ball-throwing, race-running, back-flipping boy.

Give Gage a tune and he'd make up silly rhymes for it.
Give Gage a windy day and he'd fly a kite. Give Gage a beach
and he'd build a sand castle that scraped the sky.

"That Gage!" everyone said. "He's got mojo!"

Who wouldn't love a boy like that?

But one day . . . Gage got sick. He was too sick
for ball throwing, race running, and back-flipping.
Too sick for rhymes and kites and sand castles.

And that is why his family came to the very special house in the heart of the Big City.

Like any other house, the house in the Big City has house rules:

Healthy eating
Afternoon napping
Peace and quieting
No puppies!

Meanwhile, not too far away, there was a cozy house.
It had a tiny bedroom with a boxful of chew toys. It had
a nice warm kitchen. And guess what else it had?
Puppies! A passel of puppies.

Two puppies set out to be service dogs.

Three puppies signed up for Search-and-Rescue.

Four puppies were groomed for the show ring.

And then . . . there was . . .
Mogie. Mogie was a ball-chasing,
tail-wagging, moon-howling pup.

Mogie tried to be
a service dog.

He tried Search-and-Rescue.

He even tried the show ring.

Each time, he got the same report card: no way.
No how. No, thanks.

But Mogie's heart was as true as could be.
Give that dog a puddle and he'd splash. Give him
a whistle and he'd roll over. Give him a rule and he'd
break it.
Which is exactly what he did!

When he walked through the doors of the very special house, he did not notice the high-to-the-sky ceilings and large, cushy sofas.

He could care less about the well-stocked library and the big, big kitchen.

Instead Mogie made a beeline for . . . Gage. "Arf!" he barked.

He barely sniffed the indoor tree
~~h~~ouse and the enormous fireplace. He
~~co~~mpletely ignored the rules.

Mogie trotted to Gage's side and wagged his tail,
but Gage only stared out at the sky.

Mogie rolled onto his back and kicked his legs in the air. Gage stared some more. Mogie barked in three different keys.

"That Gage!" everyone said. "He's lost his mojo."

Who wouldn't worry about a boy like that?

Not Mogie.
He knew just what to do. He licked Gage's fingers. He leaned on Gage's legs. He sat beside Gage and stared out at the big, blue sky.

And one day, when no one else was
looking, Mogie chased a ball.

He ran a race.

He did a back-flip.
Just for Gage.

And Gage? He remembered.
He remembered throwing balls ar
running races and flipping backwar
He remembered silly tunes and wind
days. One night, he dreamed about
sand castles that scraped the sky.

And slowly, slowly, oh so slowly, Gage began to get better.

The day came when Gage was ready to leave the
special house in the heart of the Big City. But first he hugged
Mogie and said, "I'll never forget you." Mogie leaned against him
and licked Gage's fingers. He barked in three different keys. Then
he watched as Gage waved good-bye and walked out the door.

Give that boy a
tree and he'll climb it.
Give him a pond and
he'll feed the ducks.
Give him a chance
and he'll take it.

"That Gage!" everyone said. "He found his mojo."

As for Mogie? He's still there, in the special house. He misses Gage, and once in a while, he stares out at the sky and thinks about him.

But now he has Antonia. Antonia was once a
toe-dancing, jump-roping, cartwheel-spinning girl.

"That Antonia!" everyone said.
"She's lost her cha-cha-cha."
Mogie's work is cut out for him.

Give this dog a bone and he'll chew it. Give him
a stick and he'll fetch it. Give him a kiddo who is
bluer than blue, and Mogie will be truer than true.

"That Mogie!" everyone said. "He's the heart of the house."

Who wouldn't love a dog like that?